LOVELY

JESS HONG

Creston Books

WHAT IS LOVELY?

LOVELY IS DIFFERENT.

BLACK.

WHITE.

TALL.

SHORT.

FLUFFY.

SLEEK.

SOFT.

SHARP.

BIG.

SMALL.

FANCY.

SPORTY.

GRACEFUL.

STOMPY.

LOVELY.

LOVELY IS DIFFERENT,
WEIRD, AND WONDERFUL.

LOVELY IS YOU.

LOVELY IS ME.

WE ARE ALL...